Sarah B.   Ms. Sniffen   Uncle Wrinkle

What's the answer? Half the fun
Is finding there is more than one.
Teachers who know this is true,
I dedicate this book to you.
  S.F.

Book design by Erik Thé
Photography by Nimkin/Parrinello

Library of Congress Cataloging-in-Publication Data Available
ISBN 0-439-11013-0

10 9 8 7 6 5 4 3 2 1   0/0 01 02 03 04

Printed in Mexico 49
First edition, September 2000

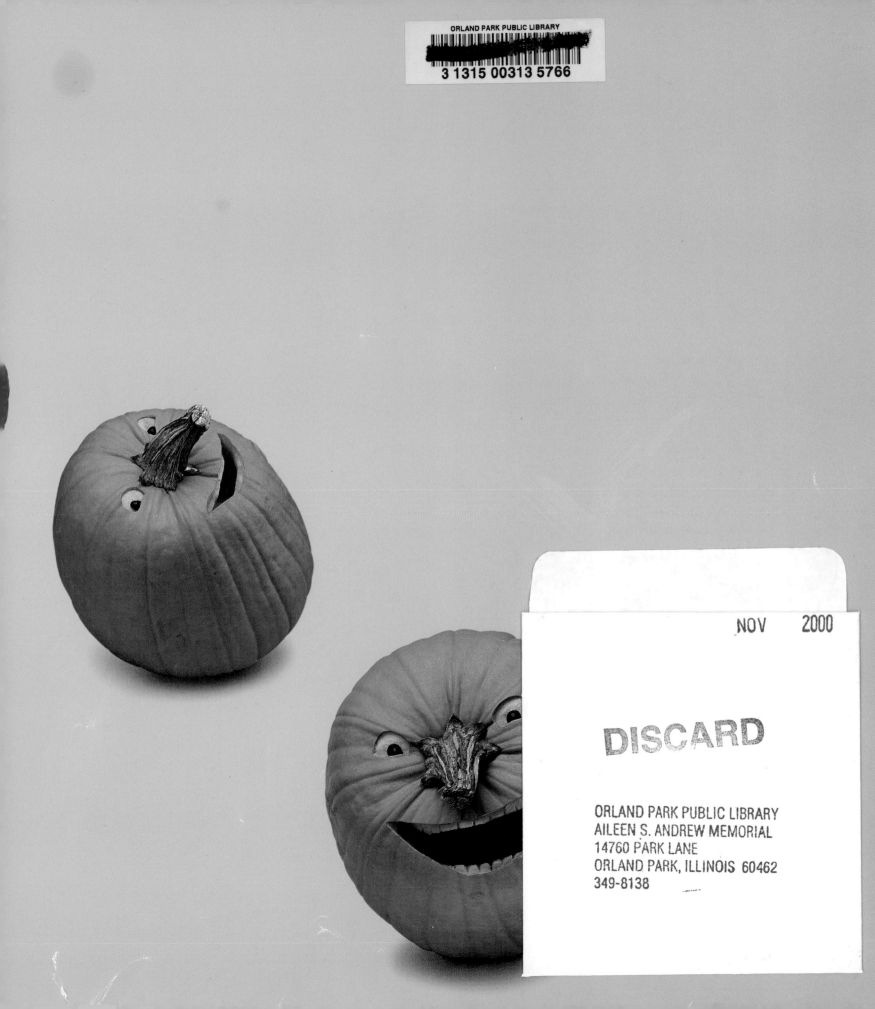

DR. POMPO'S NOSE

WRITTEN AND ILLUSTRATED BY

SAXTON FREYMANN

ARTHUR A. LEVINE BOOKS

AN IMPRINT OF SCHOLASTIC PRESS

NEW YORK

Rolling on his morning rounds,
Dr. Pompo froze.
What was that upon the ground?
Could it be a nose?

Along came Uncle Wrinkle,
who asked of Dr. P.,
"What's **that** you've got there, Pompo?
It's hard for me to see."
"It seems to be a nose, I think,"
said Pompo to his friend.
"I guess someone has lost it,
and it's standing on its end."

Wrinkle frowned. "Why Dr. P., it's nothing of the kind!
An absentminded gardener has left that thing behind.
It's a tool for gardening, as everybody knows.
Someone had to dig up weeds before they grew this rose."

Nimkin said, "I think this thing's a horn for calling sheep.
It's useful when you need them and they all have gone to sleep!"

"It's a horn, alright," laughed Jack,
"but not for blowing notes.
I've seen something just like this upon the
heads of goats!"

Mrs. Gordon disagreed.
"It's a horn to hear.
Everything sounds clearer
when you put it to your ear."

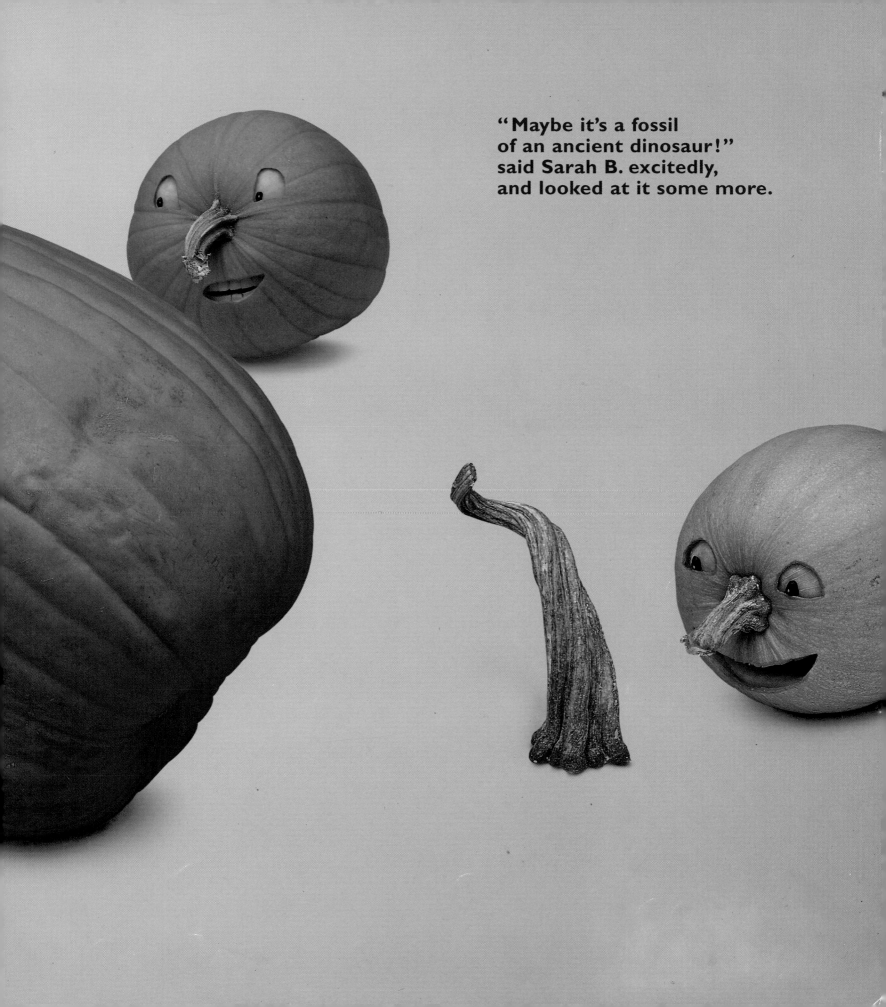

"Maybe it's a fossil
of an ancient dinosaur!"
said Sarah B. excitedly,
and looked at it some more.

"Good Hebbens!" said Ms. Sniffen, "and how do you subboze
I lost it ober dare?... Please Doctor, help be wid by doze!"

Dr. Pompo put it back,
right between her eyes.
She thanked him while the others
just looked on in dumb surprise.

"Perhaps wed I leaned ober
to sdiff dat little rose,
I sdeezed so hard I guess I bust
hab sdeezed right off by doze!"

"So," said Dr. Pompo, "Ms. Sniffen's good as new.
And I hope that all you pumpkins have learned a thing or two:
No matter what the problem, it often is the case
that the answer is as simple as the nose upon your face."